W9-CCW-580

DATE

SPRING GREEN COMMUNITY LIBRARY
230 E. Monroe Street
Spring Green, WI 53588

Parents and Caregivers,

Stone Arch Readers are designed to provide enjoyable reading experiences, as well as opportunities to develop vocabulary, literacy skills, and comprehension. Here are a few ways to support your beginning reader:

- Talk with your child about the ideas addressed in the story.

- Discuss each illustration, mentioning the characters, where they are, and what they are doing.

- Read with expression, pointing to each word. You may want to read the whole story through and then revisit parts of the story to ensure that the meanings of words or phrases are understood.

- Talk about why the character did what he or she did and what your child would do in that situation.

- Help your child connect with characters and events in the story.

Remember, reading with your child should be fun, not forced. Each moment spent reading with your child is a priceless investment in his or her literacy life.

Gail Saunders-Smith, Ph.D.

STONE ARCH **READERS**

are published by Stone Arch Books
a Capstone Imprint
151 Good Counsel Drive, P.O. Box 669
Mankato, Minnesota 56002
www.capstonepub.com

Copyright © 2010 by Stone Arch Books
All rights reserved. No part of this publication may be reproduced
in whole or in part, or stored in a retrieval system, or transmitted in any
form or by any means, electronic, mechanical, photocopying, recording,
or otherwise, without written permission of the publisher.

Printed in the United States of America in Melrose Park, Illinois.
092009
005620LKS10

Library of Congress Cataloging-in-Publication Data
Crow, Melinda Melton.
Ride and seek / by Melinda Melton Crow ; illustrated by Patrick Girouard.
p. cm. — (Stone Arch readers)
ISBN 978-1-4342-1867-4 (library binding : alk. paper)
ISBN 978-1-4342-2298-5 (pbk. : alk. paper)
[1. Trucks—Fiction.] I. Girouard, Patrick, ill. II. Title.
PZ7.C88536Ri 2010
[E]—dc22

                                        2009034288

Summary: Four truck buddies play hide-and-seek at the park.

Art Director: Kay Fraser
Graphic Designer: Hilary Wacholz
Production Specialist: Michelle Biedscheid

Reading Consultants:
Gail Saunders-Smith, Ph.D.
Melinda Melton Crow, M.Ed.
Laurie K. Holland, Media Specialist

THE SNEAKY SQUIRREL

Every time you turn the page,
look for the squirrel.

RIDE
AND
SEEK

by Melinda Melton Crow

illustrated by Patrick Girouard

STONE ARCH BOOKS
a capstone imprint

This is Tow Truck.
This is Fire Truck.
This is Green Truck.
This is Monster Truck.

Monster Truck counts.
The other trucks hide.

Fire Truck hides under
the bridge.

Green Truck hides in the forest.

Tow Truck hides in a special place.

Monster Truck says, "Ready or not, here I come!"

Monster Truck goes to look
for his pals.

"I see you, Fire Truck,"
he says.

"I see you, Green Truck,"
he says.

Monster Truck looks for
Tow Truck.

"I can't find Tow Truck,"
he says.

"Here I am," says Tow Truck.

"You are good at hiding,"
says Monster Truck.

"Now it is my turn to count," says Tow Truck.

STORY WORDS

counts under forest
hide bridge special

Total Word Count: 110

Follow your favorite TRUCK pals as they learn about the open road.